More books about
My Naughty Little Sister

My Naughty Little Sister

More Naughty Little Sister Stories

When My Naughty Little Sister Was Good

My Naughty Little Sister's Friends

My Naughty Little Sister and Bad Harry

DOROTHY EDWARDS

ILLUSTRATED BY SHIRLEY HUGHES

EGMONT

For Martine and Olivia Jane Edwards
with love

EGMONT
We bring stories to life

First published in Great Britain 1974
by Methuen Children's Books Ltd
This edition published 2014 by Dean,
an imprint of Egmont UK Limited
The Yellow Building, 1 Nicholas Road, London W11 4AN

Text copyright © 1974 The Estate of Dorothy Edwards
Illustrations copyright © 1974 Shirley Hughes
Cover illustration copyright © 2007 Shirley Hughes

The moral rights of the author and illustrator have been asserted

ISBN 978 0 6035 7033 9
58716/1
Printed in Great Britain

A CIP catalogue record for this title is available from the British Library

Printed and bound in Great Britain by the CPI Group

Contents

1. My Naughty Little Sister and Bad Harry

Once upon a time – a long time ago – when I was a little girl, I had a sister who was littler than me. Now although my sister was sometimes very naughty she had a lot of friends. Some of her friends were grown-up people but some were quite young. Her favourite child-friend was a little boy called Harry. He often made my sister cross so she called him Bad Harry.

Bad Harry lived quite near to us. There were no roads to cross to get to his house, and he and my sister often went round to visit each other without any grown-up person having to take them.

One day, when my naughty little sister went round to Bad Harry's house it was his mother's washing day. Bad Harry was very pleased to see her; he didn't like it when his mother was doing washing.

'Have you come to play?' he asked.

Now Harry's mother didn't like naughty children running about in her house while she was doing the washing, so she said, 'You'll have to play in the garden then. You know what you two are like when there's water about!'

Harry said he didn't mind that. There was a lovely game they could play in the garden. They could play *Islands*.

There was a big heap of sand at the bottom of the garden that Harry's father was going to make a path with one day. Harry said, 'We'll pretend that sand is an island in the river, like the one we go to on the ferry-boat sometimes.'

My sister said, 'Yes. We will go and live on it. We will say that all the garden is the river.'

So off they went.

They had a good game pretending
to live on the island. They filled
Harry's toy truck with sand and ran it
up and down the heap and tipped the
sand over the island's side until it
became quite flat.

Then they dug holes in the sand and stuck sticks in them and said they were planting trees.

Later on Harry went to find some more sticks and while he was gone my sister made sand-pies for their pretending dinner. My little sister made them in a flower-pot and tipped them out very carefully. They did look nice.

'Dinner time, Harry,' she said.

But instead of pretending to eat a sand pie, that bad Bad Harry knocked all the pies over with a stick.

He said, 'Now you will have to make some more.'

He thought that was a funny thing to do. But my sister didn't think so.

My naughty little sister was very, very cross with Bad Harry when he knocked her pies over. She screamed and shouted and said, 'Get off my island, bad, Bad Harry,' and she pushed him and he fell on to the garden.

When Harry fell my sister stopped being cross. She laughed instead. 'Now you're all wet in the river,' she said.

But Bad Harry didn't laugh. He was very angry.

'I'm not wet. I'm not wet,' he

shouted, and he began to jump up and down. 'You pushed me. You pushed me,' Harry said.

'You broke my pies,' shouted my sister, 'Bad old Harry,' and *she* jumped up and down too.

Bad Harry was just going to shout again when he saw something and had an idea: he saw his mother's washing-basket.

Harry's mother had filled the washing-line with sheets and she'd left the other wet things in a basket on the path so that she could hang them up when the sheets were dry.

'I've got a boat,' Harry said.

He went up to the basket with the wet things in it.

'Look,' he said. 'It's a boat!' And he began to push it along the path.

My sister forgot about being cross with Harry because she liked his idea so much. She went to help him push.

'We've got a boat,' she said.

They pushed their boat round and round the island, and they were just talking about giving each other rides in it, on top of the wet washing, and my sister was just shouting again because she wanted to be first, when Harry's mother came out.

'You are naughty children,' Harry's

mother said. 'If I hadn't caught you in time you would have got all my washing dirty. What will you do next?'

'We were playing Islands,' Bad Harry said.

'Well, you are not going to play Islands any more,' said Harry's mother. 'You will come indoors with me where I can keep an eye on you!'

'Now,' she said. 'You can each sit on a chair while I wash the kitchen floor.'

She lifted Bad Harry on to one chair, and my naughty little sister on to another chair, and she said, 'Don't you *dare* get off!'

And they *didn't* dare get off.

Harry's mother looked too cross. They didn't even talk – they were so busy watching her washing the floor.

First she used the mop on one corner. Then she picked up the chair with Bad Harry on it and put it on the wet place.

'There!' she said.

Then she washed the floor in another corner. She picked up the chair with my naughty little sister on it and put it on that wet place.

'There!' she said. 'Now don't get down till the floor is dry!'

She said, 'Curl your feet up and keep them out of the wet.'

And Bad Harry curled his feet, and my little sister curled her feet, and Bad Harry's mother laughed and said, 'Right, here I go!'

And she mopped all the floor that was left. She did it very, very quickly.

My little sister quite enjoyed watching Harry's mother mop the floor. She liked to see the mop going round and round and all the soap bubbles going round and round too. She liked to see it going backwards and forwards wiping up the bubbles. Every time the bubbles were wiped up she shouted, 'Gone away!' Our mother didn't clean *her* floor like that – so it was very interesting.

Bad Harry didn't shout though. He went very still and very quiet. He was thinking.

When Harry's mother was finished, she said, '*Well*, you *have* been good children. I'll just put some newspaper over the floor and you can get down.'

So she put newspaper all over the floor, and my little sister got down off her chair.

'Let's go and find a chocolate biscuit,' Harry's kind mother said.

My little sister smiled because she liked chocolate biscuits, but Bad Harry didn't smile. He didn't get down from his chair. He was still thinking.

He was pretending. All the time he had been on the chair he had been playing Islands. He had been pretending that the chair was an island and the wet floor was a river.

'Come on, Harry,' my naughty little sister said. 'Come and get your biscuit.'

'I can't. I'll fall in the river,' said Harry. 'I can't swim yet.'

My little sister knew at once that Harry had been playing. She looked at the wet floor with the paper all over it, then she pulled the paper across the floor and laid it in a line from Harry's chair to the door. 'Come over the bridge,' she said.

And that's what he did. And after that they made up all sorts of games with newspapers on the floor.

2. The icy cold tortoise

Long ago, when I was a little girl and had a little sister, we lived next door to a kind lady called Mrs Jones. My sister used to call this lady Mrs Cocoa sometimes.

If my mother had to go out and couldn't take my little sister this kind next-door lady used to mind her. My sister was always glad to be minded by dear Mrs Jones and Mrs Cocoa Jones was always glad to mind my little sister. They enjoyed minding days very much.

Well now, one cold blowy day when the wind was pulling all the old leaves off the trees to make room for the new baby ones to grow, our mother asked Mrs Cocoa Jones to mind my sister while she went shopping.

Mrs Cocoa and my sister had a lovely time. They swept up all the leaves from Mr Jones's nice tidy paths and put them into a heap for him to burn. They went indoors and laid Mr Jones's tea, and they were just going to sit down by the fire to have a rest when they heard Mr Cocoa coming down the back path.

Mr Cocoa came down the path

pushing his bicycle with one hand and holding a very strange-looking wooden box with holes in it in the other hand.

When Mr Jones saw my little sister peeping at him out of his kitchen window he smiled and smiled. 'Hello, Mrs Pickle,' he said. 'What are you doing here, then?'

'I'm being minded,' said my little sister. Then, because she was an inquisitive child she said, 'What have you got in that box, Mr Cocoa?'

'Just wait a minute, and I'll show you,' Mr Cocoa said, and he went off to put his bicycle in the shed.

'I wonder what's in that box, Mrs Cocoa?' said my inquisitive little sister.

'It's a very funny box – it's got holes in it.'

'Ah,' said Mrs Cocoa, 'just you wait and see!'

When kind Mr Cocoa came in and saw my impatient little sister he was so good he didn't even stop to take off his coat. He opened the box at *once* – and he showed my sister an icy-cold tortoise, lying fast asleep under a lot of hay.

Have you ever seen a tortoise? My little sister hadn't.

Tortoises are very strange animals. They have hard round shells and long crinkly necks and little beaky noses.

They have tiny black eyes and four scratchy-looking claws.

But when they are asleep you can't see their heads or their claws; they are tucked away under their shells. They just look like cold round stones.

My little sister thought the tortoise was a stone at first. She touched it, and it was icy-cold. 'What is it?' she said. 'What is this stone-thing?'

Mr Cocoa picked the tortoise up and showed her where the little claws were tucked away, and the beaky little shut-eyed face under the shell.

'It's a tortoise,' Mr Cocoa said.

'He's having his winter sleep now,'

said Mrs Cocoa.

Mr Jones told my sister that one of the men who worked with him had given him the tortoise, because he was going away and wouldn't have anywhere to keep it in his new home.

'I shall put him away in the cupboard under the stairs now,' he said. 'He will sleep there all the winter and wake up again when the warm days come.'

Just as Mr Cocoa said this, the tortoise opened its little beady black eyes and looked at my sister. Then it closed them and went to sleep again. So Mr Cocoa put it away in its box right at the back of the cupboard under the stairs.

'That's a funny animal,' my naughty little sister said.

After that, she talked and talked about the tortoise. She kept saying, 'When will it wake up? – When will it wake up?' But it didn't so she got tired of asking. By the time Christmas came she had almost forgotten it. And when the snow fell she quite forgot it.

And when spring came and the birds began to sing again, and she went in one day to have her morning cocoa with her next-door friend, Mrs Jones had forgotten it too!

They were just drinking their cocoa and Mrs Jones was telling my naughty little sister about some of the things she had done when she was a little girl when they heard:

Thump! Thump! Bang! Bang!

'Oh dear,' said Mrs Cocoa. 'There's someone at the front door!' And she went to look. But there wasn't.

Thump! Thump!

'It must be the back door,' said Mrs Cocoa Jones, and she went to look but it wasn't!

Bang! Bang!

'What can it be?' asked Mrs Jones.

Now, my clever little sister had been

listening hard. 'It's in the under-the-stairs place, Mrs Cocoa,' she said. 'Listen.'

Thump! Thump! Bang! Bang!

'Oh goodness,' said Mrs Cocoa. But she was a very brave lady. She opened the door of the cupboard and looked and my little sister looked too.

And Mrs Cocoa stared and my little sister stared.

There was the tortoise's wooden box, shaking and bumping because the cross tortoise inside had woken up and was banging to be let out.

'Goodness me,' said Mrs Cocoa. 'That tortoise has woken up!'

'Goodness me,' said my funny sister. 'That tortoise has woken up!'

And Mrs Cocoa looked hard at my sister and my sister looked hard at her.

'I shall have to see to it,' Mrs Cocoa said, and she picked up the bumping box and carried it into her kitchen and put the box on the table. Then she lifted my sister up to the chair so she could watch.

Mrs Cocoa lifted the lid off the box, and there was that wide-awake tortoise. His head was waggle-waggling and his claws scratch-scratching to get out.

'I used to have a tortoise when I

was a girl,' Mrs Cocoa said, 'so I know just what to do!'

And do you know what she did? She put some warm water into a bowl, and she put the tortoise in the warm water. Then she took it out and dried it very, very carefully on an old soft towel.

Then Mrs Cocoa put the clean fresh tortoise on the table, and said, 'Just mind it while I go and get it something to eat, there's a good child. Just put your hand gently on his back and he will stay quite still.'

My little sister did keep her hand on the tortoise's back and he was quite still until Mrs Cocoa came back with a cabbage leaf.

'Look,' my naughty little sister said,
'look at his waggly head, Mrs Jones.'

And she put her face right down so she could see his little black eyes. 'Hello, Mister Tortoise,' she said.

And the tortoise made a funny noise at her. It said, 'His-ss-SS.'

My poor sister was surprised! She didn't like that noise very much. But Mrs Cocoa said the tortoise had only said, 'His-ss-SS' because it was hungry and not because it was cross. Mrs Cocoa said tortoises are nice friendly things so long as you let them go their own way.

And because my little sister had minded the tortoise for her she let her give him the cabbage leaf.

At first he only looked at it, and pushed it about with his beaky head, but at last he bit a big piece out of it.

'There!' Mrs Jones said. 'That's the first thing he's tasted since last summer!'

Just fancy that!

Mr Cocoa made the tortoise a little home in his rockery where it could sleep, and it could walk around among the stones or hide among the rockery flowers if it wanted to.

Sometimes it used to eat the flowers, and make Mr Cocoa cross.

That tortoise lived with the Cocoa Joneses for many, many years. It slept under the stairs in the winter and walked about the rockery in summer. It was still there when my sister was a grown-up lady.

Mr and Mrs Cocoa called it Henry, but of course when my sister was little she always called it Henry Cocoa Jones.

3. My Naughty Little Sister and Bad Harry at the library

Nowadays libraries are very nice places where there are plenty of picture-books for children to look at, and a very nice lady who will let you take some home to read so long as you promise not to tear them or scribble in them.

When I was a little girl we had a library in the town where we lived. Our mother used to go there once a week to get a book to read, and when I was old enough I used to go with her to get a book for myself.

Our library wasn't as nice as the one nearest to your house. There wasn't a special children's part. The children's books were in a corner among the grown-up books, and all the books had dark brown library-covers – no nice bright picture-covers. You had to look inside them to find out what the stories were about.

Still, when I did look, I found some very good stories just as you do nowadays.

But we didn't have very nice people to give out the books.

There was a cross old man with glasses who didn't like children very much. When we brought our book back he would look through it very carefully to make sure we hadn't messed it up and grumble if he found a spot or a tear – even if it was nothing to do with us.

And there was a lady who used to say, 'Sh-sh-sh' all the time, and come and grumble if you held one book while you were looking at another one. She would say, 'All books to be returned to the shelves immediately.'

My little sister went to the library with us once, but she said she wouldn't come any more because she didn't like the shushy lady and the glasses man.

So after that Mrs Cocoa Jones minded her on library days.

So, you can imagine how surprised we were one day when she said, 'I want to go the library.'

Our mother said, 'But you don't like the library. You're always saying how nasty it is there.'

But my little sister said, 'Yes, I do. I do like it *now*.'

She said, 'I don't want to go with you though, I want to go with Bad Harry's mother.'

What a surprise!

Our mother said, 'I don't suppose Harry's mother wants to take *you*. It must be hard enough for her with Harry.'

But, do you know, Harry's mother *did* want to take my sister. Bad Harry's mother said, '*Please* let her come with us. Harry has been worrying and worrying to ask you.'

So my mother said my little sister could go to the library with Bad Harry and his mother, but she said she thought she had better come along too.

'I don't trust those two bad children when they're together,' our mother said.

All the way to the library those naughty children walked in front of their mothers whispering and giggling together, and our mother said, 'I just hope they won't get up to mischief.'

But Harry's mother said, 'Oh no! *Harry is always as quiet as a mouse in the library.*'

Bad Harry – quiet as a mouse! Fancy that.

But so he was. And so was my sister. They were both as quiet as two mice.

When they got to the library, the man with glasses wasn't cross, he said, 'Hello, sonny,' to Bad Harry and that was a surprise. (But of course at that time Harry still looked good.)

And then the shushing lady came

along. She smiled at Harry, and Harry smiled at her, and the lady looked at my naughty little sister and said, 'We don't mind good children like Harry coming here!'

My little sister was very surprised, and so was my mother, but Harry's mother said, 'Harry is always good in the library. He goes and sits in the little book-room in the corner, and he doesn't make a sound until I'm ready to go!'

Harry's mother said, 'He looks at the books on the table and he is as good as gold.'

Of course our mother was worried because she thought my sister couldn't be like that, but she let my sister go with Harry while she went to find herself a new book to read.

And, do you know, all the time our mother and Harry's mother were choosing books those children were quiet as mice.

And when our mother and Harry's mother were ready to go, there they were sitting good as gold, looking at a book in the little book-room.

When our mother got home she said, 'I would never have believed it. Those children were like *angels*!'

So after that my naughty little sister often went to the library with

Bad Harry and his mother. And they were always quiet as mice.

Then one day Bad Harry's mother found out why.

One day when they were in the library she found a book very quickly, and, when she went along to the little book-room she had a great surprise. She couldn't see them anywhere!

Then she looked again, and there they were – under the book-table.

They were lying very still on their tummies, staring at something, and, as Harry's mother bent down to see what they were doing, a tiny mouse ran over the floor and into a hole in the wall!

You see, the very first time Harry had visited the library, he had seen that little mouse, and afterwards he always looked out for it.

He used to take things for it to eat sometimes: pieces of cheese and bacon-rind. The mouse had been Bad Harry's secret friend, and now it was my sister's secret friend too.

Harry's mother told our mother all about those funny children and the library mouse. She said, 'I suppose I ought to tell the librarian.'

But our mother said, 'I don't see why. That old man is always nibbling biscuits. He keeps them under the counter. He just encourages mice.'

I hadn't known about the biscuit nibbling, but the next time I went to get a book I peeped, and Mother was right. There was a bag of biscuits under the cross man's counter and piles of biscuit crumbs!

No wonder there was a library

mouse. And no
wonder it made
friends with
Bad Harry.
The cheese and bacon
bits must have been a great change
from biscuit crumbs, mustn't they?

4. Grandad's special holly

In the long time ago when I was a little girl with a naughty little sister, we had a dear old grandad who had two gardens. He had a pretty little garden round his house with flowers and apples in it, and a big garden near the park for vegetables. The garden near the park was called an allotment. It had a tall hedge at the bottom of it, and in this tall hedge was a big tree with green-and-white leaves. It was a very, very prickly tree.

We used to go and see Grandad

when he was working on his allotment. We used to take him something to drink because he said digging made him thirsty. In summer he had a jug of cold tea and in winter he had a jug of hot cocoa. In summer he would sit on his wheelbarrow and drink his tea and talk to us and in the wintertime we used to go into his allotment shed and warm our hands by the oil-stove while he drank his cocoa.

One day, when Grandad was drinking cold tea and the sun was shining, my little sister said, 'I don't like your prickly tree very much, Grandad. It prickled my fingers.'

Grandad said, 'That's a very special tree, that is. That's a variegated holly-tree. You don't see trees like that every day.' He said it in a very proud way.

He said, 'When Christmas-time comes it will be full of red berries.'

Then he told us that every Christmas Eve he would bring a ladder and climb up the holly-tree and cut off some of its beautiful green-and-white branches with the red berries. He would put the cut holly into his wheelbarrow and take it down to the Church.

Every Christmas Eve afternoon he

took his holly to the Church so the church-ladies could hang it up on the walls and make them look nice for Christmas.

Grandad said, 'When I go to Church on Christmas Morning, I like to look up and see the greenery. I can always pick out my holly, it's special.'

When my little sister told our father about the holly he said he remembered how when he was a little boy he used to go with Grandad to take the Church-holly on Christmas Eve. He said he could still remember going through the town with all the people pointing and saying, 'Look at the lovely holly!'

My little sister was pleased to hear about our father being a little boy and going to the Church with Grandad and the holly, and the next time we went to the allotment she told Grandad *she* would like to go with him on Christmas Eve.

And Grandad said well, if Mother didn't mind he'd be very pleased to take her when Christmas Eve came.

Our mother said she didn't mind a bit, because she knew Grandad would take great care of my sister. She said when Christmas Eve came if she still wanted to go with Grandad it would be quite all right.

'Christmas Eve is a long way off,' our mother said. 'You may change your mind by then.'

But my naughty little sister *didn't* change her mind. Every time she saw Grandad she said, 'How are the holly-berries?' And when he showed her how they were growing and how red they were getting she got very impatient.

She kept saying, 'Will it soon be Christmas?' She was so afraid our dear old grandad would forget and take the holly without her.

But he didn't. On the very next Christmas Eve, just after we'd eaten our dinner there was a loud knock on the front-door, and when Mother opened it – there was Grandad smiling and smiling and outside the gate was his great big wheelbarrow piled high with the lovely green-and-white and red-berried holly.

Some of the people in the road were looking out of their windows, and while our mother was putting my sister's warm coat on and tying the red woolly scarf round her neck, a lady came to our door and asked if Grandad would sell her some holly.

Grandad said, 'No, I'm very sorry, all this is for the Church.' But he gave the lady a little piece for her Christmas pudding and the lady was very glad to have it. My little sister said the lady's pudding would look very grand with special holly on it, and the lady said she was sure it would.

Now it was a long walk to the Church, so our grandad said my little sister had better ride on the wheelbarrow. He had put some sacks in front of the barrow over the prickly leaves, and my little sister climbed on and sat down, and off they went.

My naughty little sister *did* enjoy that ride, even though the holly prickles poked through the sacks and

scratched her a little bit. It was just like Father had said. All the people stared and said, 'What lovely holly!' and smiled at my little sister with her holly-berry red scarf sitting in front of Grandad's wheelbarrow.

They had to go down the High Street where the shops were because the Church was there too, and a man who sold oranges gave my sister one. He said, 'Happy Christmas, ducks,' to her as she went by. Wasn't that nice of him? My sister thought it was and so did Grandad.

When they got to the Church the ladies all came out to look at

Grandad's big load of variegated holly.

Grandad said, 'Lift it carefully, we don't want the berries knocked off.'

While Grandad and some of the ladies were taking the branches inside, one of the ladies talked to my little sister. She said, 'Would you like to come and see the manger?'

My little sister knew about 'Way in a Manger' and about Baby Jesus being born at Christmas-time, so although she didn't know what the lady meant she said, 'Yes,' because she knew it would be something nice.

And so it was.

That kind lady took my little sister

into the cold grey church where a lot of people were making it look bright and Christmassy with holly and ivy and white flowers in pots. My naughty little sister wanted to stop and look at a man on a ladder who was handing up some Christmas-tree branches, but the lady said, 'Come on.'

Then she said, 'There! It's just finished. Isn't it pretty?'

And there, in a corner of the cold old church someone had built a wooden shed with a manger with straw in it inside. There was a statue of Mary and a statue of Joseph standing on each side of the manger, and on the straw inside it was a little stony Baby Jesus statue.

There was a picture of an ox and a donkey on the wall at the back of the shed, and round the shed doorway were pictures of angels.

My little sister said, 'My grandad's got a shed like that on his allotment. He's got a stove in it though.'

And she looked very hard at the Mary statue and the Joseph statue and the Baby Jesus statue.

The lady said, 'The Sunday School children always bring toys to Church on Christmas Day to send to the children in hospital. They leave them by the manger because that's where the shepherds put their presents.' The lady said that tomorrow morning there would be some shepherd statues by the manger too.

Then she said, 'You can stay and look if you like. I'll just go and help your grandaddy to break up some of the holly branches.'

So my naughty little sister stayed there, looking and looking. It was very cold in that big church. Mary looked cold and Joseph looked cold too. Very, very carefully my little sister leaned into the shed and touched the little Baby Jesus statue and he was cold as ice!

My naughty little sister stayed by the manger for a little while longer and then she went to find Grandad who was ready to go home. There was lots of room in the wheelbarrow now, and lots more things to see on the way home, but my little sister was very, very quiet.

And what do you think happened?

The next day, which was Christmas Day of course, when I went with the other Sunday School boys and girls to leave a present by the manger for the ill children, we saw a very strange thing.

There were Mary and Joseph. The Shepherds were there too. And there was the little Baby Jesus!

But the little Baby Jesus wasn't cold any more. He was wrapped up in my naughty little sister's red woolly scarf, and he had an orange beside him!

The Sunday School teacher said, 'Your funny little sister did that last night! Wasn't that sweet of her? She thought he was cold!'

5. Granny's wash-day

Long ago, when I was a little girl with a naughty little sister we had two grannies. We had a granny who lived near us and a granny in the country.

We could see our near-granny whenever we wanted to, but we only saw our country-granny when we could go and stay with her.

Our country-granny lived in a pretty house with roses all over it. It was a funny house. One of the funny things about it was that there were no taps in it at all.

There was a big pump in the back garden. This pump was on top of a deep well full of clear cold water. Our granny got all her water out of that well.

One time my naughty little sister went to stay with this granny and she liked it very much. There were five kind uncles living there too and they made a great fuss of my little sister.

But although these uncles were so kind they made such a lot of noise and needed such a lot of looking-after and ate such very big dinners that my little sister said, 'I shan't have any boys when I'm a lady.'

Every day our granny cooked big dinners for all the hungry uncles. Every day our hungry uncles ate all the big dinners up. On *Sunday* Granny cooked such a *big*, *big* dinner that my little sister said, 'Do the uncles eat more than ever because it's Sunday?'

'Oh, no, my dear,' our granny said. 'I always cook extra potatoes and extra cabbage for *bubble-and-squeak*. Tomorrow is wash-day,' Granny said. 'I don't have time for much cooking on wash-day.'

When Granny said 'bubble-and-squeak' my little sister laughed. She hadn't heard about bubble-and-squeak before. So she said it lots of times. She said, 'Bubble-and-squeak, bubble-and-squeak,' over and over again. It sounded so bubbly and so squeaky when she said it to herself that she could hardly stop laughing at all.

When my little sister *did* stop laughing she asked what 'bubble-and-squeak' was. But our granny said, 'Wait until tomorrow and then you can taste some.'

(Do you know what bubble-and-squeak is? If you don't you'll know at the end of the story.)

Well, next day was Monday and Monday was wash-day at our granny's house.

Our granny's wash-day was a very busy day. Everyone got up very, very early. Even my little sister. She heard all the people moving about and she got up to see what they were doing.

Our uncles carried lots of large pails out to the garden, and pumped up water and filled all the pails up to the top. Then those kind men carried all the heavy pails back to the house and left them by the back door. They wanted to help their mother so they fetched all the water for wash-day before they had their breakfasts.

When our uncles had gone off to work my little sister helped Granny too. She helped Granny collect all the dirty things that had to be washed.

My little sister liked helping to do this. It was great fun. Granny took all the sheets and pillow-cases off the beds and all the towels and our uncles' dirty shirts and things and she put them outside the bedroom doors. Then my little sister took all the sheets and pillow-cases and towels and all the other things from outside the bedroom doors and *she threw them all down the stairs*. And she wasn't being naughty.

She threw them down the stairs because Granny said it saved carrying them down.

It was very nice throwing the dirty things down the stairs and my little sister was sorry when there was nothing left to throw. But she was a good child. She went downstairs with Granny and helped her to carry the things out to the wash-house next to the back-door.

Do you know what a wash-house is? I will tell you what our granny's wash-house was like. It was a long room. In a corner there was a big copper for boiling the water. There was a fire burning under the copper to make the water hot. There was a big sink and lots of big baths full of cold water for rinsing the washing.

Granny had a big wringer for wringing the wet clothes in her wash-house. She had some clothes lines too. She had them hanging up in the wash-house in case it rained on wash-day.

A lady called Mrs Apple came to help Granny do her washing. She had a brown apron on with a big pocket in front of it, and this big pocket was full of pegs.

My little sister had never seen such a big wash-day before. She was so

interested she got in Granny's way. She got in Mrs Apple's way too. Mrs Apple dipped a funny little bag full of blue stuff into one of the baths full of water and made the water blue, and my naughty little sister liked it so much she splashed and dabbled in it and got herself wet.

Granny said, 'Oh dear, you're as bad as your mother used to be on wash-days when she was your age.'

My sister was surprised to hear that our mother had been a naughty little girl when she was little.

Kind Mrs Apple said, 'Ah, but your mummy was a good girl too. Now, see if you can be a good girl.' And she gave my little sister a basin full of warm water and let her wash her own cotton socks and handkerchiefs. Mrs Apple said, 'It will be a great help if you do those.'

So my little sister rubbed and rubbed and when they were as clean as they could be, kind Mrs Apple let her put them into the big copper for boiling.

She held my little sister up so that she could drop the socks and handkerchiefs in for herself. Then Mrs Apple put more wood on the copper fire and said, 'They will all cook nicely now.'

Then Mrs Apple washed and washed and our granny rinsed and rinsed. The wringer was turned and the water ran out of the clothes. The copper steamed and steamed and my little sister was so interested and got in the way so much that at last our granny said, 'I know what I will do with you. I will do the same thing I used to do to your mother and your uncles when they got in the way on wash-days.'

What do you think that was? It was something very nice. Our granny went to a shelf and took down a little chair-swing with strong ropes on it. Then she climbed up on a chair and my little sister saw that there were two big hooks in the wash-house roof. Granny put the ropes over the hooks. She tried the swing with her hands to make sure it was safe and strong and then she lifted my naughty little sister into the swing and gave it a big push.

My little sister had a lovely time swinging in the steamy splashy wash-house. Now she was not in the way at all and she could see everything that was happening.

Sometimes Granny gave her a little push. Sometimes Mrs Apple pushed. Sometimes my little sister swung herself.

My little sister sang and sang and
Mrs Apple said it was nice to hear her.
She said my little sister sounded just
like a dickey-bird.

When the washing was quite
finished, Granny lifted my little sister
out of the swing, and then Granny and

Mrs Apple and my little sister all had cups of cocoa and bread-and-cheese. My little sister was very hungry because she had got up so early. Granny and Mrs Apple were hungry because they had worked so hard.

After that they all went into the garden where there were more clothes-lines, and my little sister held the peg basket for Granny while she pegged out the sheets. Mrs Apple had pegs in her pocket so she didn't have to hold out the basket for her.

There were three long clothes-lines in Granny's garden and when the sheets and towels and shirts and things were blowing in the wind my sister saw what a lot of washing they had done. She was very glad to see the socks and handkerchiefs she had washed blowing too.

Then Mrs Apple went off to her own house to get her husband's dinner.

'*Now*,' said Granny, 'I shall cook that bubble-and-squeak. Come and watch me and then when you grow up you will know how to make it for yourself.'

First Granny put a lot of meaty-looking dripping into a big black frying-pan. She put the pan on top of the stove. The fat got very hot, and when it was hot it was all runny and bubbly. Then Granny took the cold potatoes and the cold cabbage that she had cooked on Sunday, and she put them all into the pan.

Granny cooked the potatoes and the cabbage in the hot fat until they were a lovely goldy-brown colour.

'The bubble-and-squeak is finished now,' Granny said, and she put it on a hot plate and popped it into the oven to keep warm, until our uncles came home for dinner.

It was very nice indeed! My naughty little sister said so and so did our hungry uncles. My little sister ate and ate and the uncles ate and ate.

My little sister said, 'Can I have some more bubble-and-squeak, please?' when she had finished her first lot.

'Why, you eat more than we do,' our uncles said.

'Yes,' said my naughty little sister, 'but I have been working hard today and it's made me very hungry.'

She said, 'I think bubble-and-squeak is the best wash-day dinner in the world.'

6. Crusts

A long time ago, when my sister was a little girl, she didn't like eating bread-and-butter crusts.

Our mother was very cross about this, because she had to eat crusts when she was a little girl, and she thought my sister should eat her crusts up too!

Every day at tea-time, Mother would put a piece of bread-and-butter on our plates and say, '*Plain* first. *Jam* second, and *cake if you're lucky*!'

She would say '*Plain* first. *Jam*

second, and *cake if you're lucky*,' because that is what our granny used to say to her when she was a little girl.

That meant that we ought to eat plain bread-and-butter before we had some with jam on, and all the bread – even the crusts – or we wouldn't get any cake.

I always ate my piece of bread-and-butter up straight away like a good girl, but my naughty little sister didn't. She used to bend her piece in half and nibble out the middle soft part and leave the crust on her plate.

Sometimes she played games with the crust – she would hold it up and peep through the hole and say, 'I see you.'

Sometimes she would put her hand through it and say, 'I've got a wrist-watch!' And sometimes she would break it up into little pieces and leave them all over the tablecloth. But she never, never ate it. Wasn't she a wasteful child?

Then, when she'd stopped playing with her bread-and-butter crust my bad little sister would say, 'Cake.'

'Cake,' she would say. 'Cake – *please.*'

Our mother would say, 'What about that crust? Aren't you going to eat it?'

And my naughty little sister would shake her head. 'All messy. Nasty crust,' she would say.

'No crust. No cake,' Mother said. But it didn't make any difference though. My bad sister said, 'I'll get down then!' And if anyone tried to make her eat her crust she would scream and scream.

Our mother didn't know what to do. She told Mrs next-door Cocoa Jones and Mrs Cocoa said, 'Try putting something nice on the crusts. See if she will eat them then!'

Mrs Cocoa said, 'She loves pink fishpaste, try that.'

So next day at tea-time our mother said, 'Will you eat your crusts up if I put pink fish-paste on them?'

And my naughty little sister said, 'Oh, *pink* fish-paste!' because that was a very great treat. 'I like pink fish-paste,' my sister said.

So our mother put some pink fish-paste on the crust that my little sister had left.

'*Now* eat it up,' Mother said.

But my sister didn't eat her crust after all. No. Do you know what she did? She licked all the fish-paste off her crust and then she put it back on her plate and said, 'Finished. No cake. Get down now.'

Wasn't she a naughty girl?

One day during the time when my sister wouldn't eat crusts Bad Harry and his mother came to tea at our house.

When Bad Harry's mother saw that my little sister wasn't eating her crusts she was very surprised. She said, 'Why aren't you eating your crusts?'

My sister said, 'I don't like them.'

Bad Harry's mother said, 'But you always eat your crusts when you come

to our house. You eat them all up then, just like Harry does.'

We were amazed when we heard Bad Harry's mother say that. She said, 'They don't leave crust or crumb!' But my naughty little sister didn't say anything and Bad Harry didn't say anything either.

When our father came home from work and Mother told him about my sister eating her crusts at Harry's house, Father was very stern.

'That shows you've got to be firm with that child,' he said, and he shook his finger at my sister.

'No more crusts left on plates. I

mean it.' He did look cross.

And my naughty little sister said in a tiny little voice, 'No crusts like Harry? No crusts like Bad Harry.'

And Father said, 'No crusts like Good Harry. No crusts or *I will know the reason why.*'

So after that there were no more crusts on my little sister's plate and she ate cake after that like everyone else.

But one day, a long time afterwards when our mother was spring-cleaning, she was dusting under the table, and saw some funny green mossy-stuff growing out from a crack underneath the table-top.

This crack belonged to a little drawer that had lost its handle and hadn't been opened for a long time.

Mother said, 'Goodness. What on earth is that?' And she went and fetched something to hook into the drawer, and then she tried to pull it out. It took a long time because the drawer was stuck.

Mother pulled and prodded and tapped and all of a sudden the drawer rushed out so quickly it fell on to the floor.

And all over the floor was a pile of green mouldy crusts!

My naughty little sister had found

that crack under the table and pushed all her crusts into the drawer when no one was looking!

My sister was very surprised to see all that mossy-looking old bread. She had forgotten all about it.

When Mother scolded her she said, 'I must have been very naughty. I eat my crusts now though, don't I?'

'And we thought you were being good like Harry,' our mother said, and then my sister laughed and laughed.

And do you want to know why she did that? Well, a long time after that, Harry's father got the gas-men to put a new stove in their kitchen, and when the gas-men took the old gas-cooker out they found lots and lots of old dried-up crusts behind it.

When our mother heard about this, she laughed too. 'Fancy us expecting you to learn anything *good* from that Bad Harry,' she said.

7. My Naughty Little Sister and the ring

A long time ago, when I was a little girl and my sister was a very, very little girl she was always putting things into her mouth to see what they tasted like.

Even things that weren't meant to be tasted. And even though our mother had told her over and over again that it was a naughty thing to do.

Our mother would say, 'Look at that child! She's got something in her mouth *again*!'

She would pick my sister up and say, 'Now, now, Baby, give it to Mother.'

And my naughty little sister would take it out of her mouth and put it into Mother's hand.

My sister tasted all sorts of silly things; pennies, pencils, nails, pebbles – things like that.

Our mother said, 'One day you will swallow something like this, and then you *will* have a tummy-ache!'

But do you know, even though my sister didn't want to have a tummy-ache she *still* put things in her mouth!

Our mother said, 'It is a very bad habit.'

Well now, one day, a lady called Mrs Clarke came to tea with us. Mrs

Clarke was very fond of children, and when she saw my little sister all neat and tidied up for the visit, she said, 'What a dear little girl.'

Now, my little sister was quite a shy child, and sometimes when people came to our house she would hide behind our mother's skirt. But when Mrs Clarke said she was a dear little girl, and when she saw what a nice lady Mrs Clarke was, she smiled at her at once and went and sat on her lap when she asked her to.

Mrs Clarke played 'Ride a cock horse' with my little sister. Then she took my sister's fat little hand and played 'Round and round the garden' on it. Then she told my sister a funny little poem and made her laugh. My naughty little sister *did* like Mrs Clarke.

She liked her so much that when Mrs Clarke and our mother started talking to each other, she stayed on Mrs Clarke's lap and was as good as gold.

First my sister looked up at Mrs Clarke's nice powdery face. Then she twisted round and looked at the pretty flowers on Mrs Clarke's dress. There were some sparkly buttons on Mrs Clarke's dress too.

My sister touched all those sparkly buttons to see if they were hard or soft and then she turned again and looked at Mrs Clarke's hands.

When Mrs Clarke talked she waved and waved her hands, and my naughty little sister saw there was something very sparkly indeed on one of Mrs Clarke's fingers.

My sister said, 'Button. Pretty button,' and tried to get hold of it.

Our mother said, 'Why, she thinks it's one of your buttons!'

Mrs Clarke said, 'It's a ring, dear. It's my diamond ring. Would you like to see it?' and she took the ring off her

finger so that my little sister could hold it.

The diamond ring was very, very sparkly indeed. My little sister turned it and turned it, and lots of shiny lights came out of it in all directions. Sometimes the lights were white and sometimes they had colours in them. My sister couldn't stop looking at it.

Mrs Clarke said my sister could mind her ring for a little while, and then she and Mother started talking again.

Presently my little sister began to wonder if the ring would taste as sparkly as it looked. It was sparklier than fizzy lemonade. So of course she put the ring in her mouth, and of course it didn't taste like lemonade at all.

After that my sister listened to

Mother and Mrs Clarke talking.

Mrs Clarke was a funny lady and she said things that made our mother laugh, and although my sister didn't know what she was laughing about, my sister began to laugh too, and Mrs Clarke hugged her and said she was a 'funny little duck'.

It was very nice until Mrs Clarke said, 'Well, I must think about going home soon,' because then she said, 'I'll have to have my ring back now, lovey.'

And the ring wasn't there.

It wasn't in my sister's hand. It wasn't on the table, or on the floor. *And it wasn't in my sister's mouth either.*

Our mother said, 'Did you put it in your mouth?' and she looked at my sister very hard.

And my sister said, in a tiny, tiny voice, 'Yes.'

Then our mother said, 'She must have swallowed it.' Mother looked so worried when she said this, that my sister got very frightened and began to scream.

She remembered what Mother had said about swallowing things that weren't meant to be eaten. She said, 'Oh! Oh! Tummy-ache! Tummy-ache!'

But Mrs Clarke said, 'It wouldn't be in your tummy yet, you know.' The

sensible lady said, 'We'll take you

along to the doctor's.'

But my sister went on crying and shouting, 'Swallowed it. Swallowed it.'

No one could stop her.

Then Father came home. When he heard the noise he was quite astonished. He shouted, 'Quiet, quiet,' to my sister in such a bellowy voice that she stopped at once.

Then Father said, 'What's all the fuss about?' and our mother told him.

Father looked at my little sister, and then he looked at Mrs Clarke. He stared very hard at Mrs Clarke and then he laughed and laughed.

'Look,' he said, 'Look – look at Mrs Clarke's button.'

Mrs Clarke looked, Mother looked and even my frightened little sister looked, and there was the ring hanging on one of Mrs Clarke's shiny buttons!

My silly little sister had taken it out of her mouth and hung it on to one of Mrs Clarke's dress-buttons to see which was the most glittery, and then she had forgotten all about it.

When our mother had said she must have swallowed it, my sister really thought she had.

She'd even thought she had a tummy-ache.

And she'd screamed and made a fuss.

What a silly child.

Father and Mother and Mrs Clarke laughed and laughed and laughed – they were so glad my naughty little sister hadn't swallowed the ring after all!

My sister didn't laugh though, she hid her face in Mother's lap and wouldn't come out again until Mrs Clarke had gone home.

But she never put anything in her mouth again – except the right things of course, like food and sweeties, and *toothbrushes*!

8. Harry's very bad day

When my naughty little sister's friend Harry was a very little boy he was often bad without knowing it. I expect you used to be like that sometimes.

Once Harry had a day being bad like that.

One day, when his mother was busy cleaning her house and his father was busy sawing wood in the garden Harry climbed up on to a chair in the kitchen and began to bang a spoon on a plate.

Harry sometimes banged his spoon

on the plate after he had eaten his dinner and nobody had grumbled at him. But Harry's dinner-plate was the sort that doesn't break.

This day Harry banged a spoon on one of his mother's best china dinner-plates. It made a much nicer noise than Harry's own plate did so he hit it harder and harder. Presently he hit it on the edge, and it jumped and fell off the table on to the hard kitchen floor.

And of course it broke.

Bad Harry said, 'Broke!' in a very surprised voice.

Then he said, 'Broke it. Broke it all up.'

'*Broke it*,' he shouted and his mother heard him and came and grumbled at him.

'Oh Harry, you are a bad, bad boy,' she said. 'I can't take my eyes off you for one minute.'

Harry said, 'Plate broke. All fall down.'

'Yes, and *you* broke it,' said Harry's mother. 'It was very, very naughty.'

She said, 'I can't watch you all the time. You had better go out in the garden and watch Daddy. He is making me some new shelves.'

So Bad Harry took his spoon and went out into the garden to see what his father was doing.

'Stand there if you want to watch,' Harry's father said. 'Don't come any nearer or you might get sawn by mistake, and you wouldn't like that.'

So Bad Harry stood still and

watched.

Harry's father had a plank of wood on his bench and he was sawing.

Zzzz-zzz, Zzzz-zzz went the saw, and all the yellow sawdust fell on to the ground.

Zzzz-zzz, Zzzz-zzz, Zzzz-zzz went the bright shining saw, and then, plunk! a piece of wood fell off.

'Another shelf cut,' Harry's father said, and he took it indoors to measure it against the kitchen wall. He took the saw too. He didn't want Harry to play with that.

But Harry didn't want to play with the saw anyway. He wanted to play with the heap of yellow sawdust.

First he put his foot in it, and pushed it round and made it all swirly.

Then he knelt down and put his spoon in it. He tried to taste it, but it was nasty and stuck to his tongue, so he spat it out again. Then he threw spoonfuls of sawdust up in the air. It blew all over the flowerbed. 'There it goes,' Harry said.

'There it goes,' and he threw some more. He liked doing that.

Presently, he dropped his spoon and picked up two big, big handfuls of sawdust and threw it up in the air at once, but it didn't blow away – it all came down on his head! It got all mixed up in his curls.

But Harry didn't mind. He threw up some more sawdust and began to laugh.

'Up in the air,' he said. 'Up in the air.'

He thought it was a very nice game.

Harry's father was very cross when he came out and saw the mess on his flowerbeds; he didn't think it was a nice game; he shouted at Harry.

Harry's mother was very cross when she saw all the sawdust in Harry's hair. She had to brush it out at once.

'I suppose you'd better come with *me*,' Harry's mother said and she took him upstairs with her, and sat him on the floor and found him some toys to play with. 'Now behave yourself,' she said, and went back to polish the floor again.

But Bad Harry didn't like those toys very much – he didn't want to play with them at all. He wanted to help his mother do her work.

So he went across the room and he found a big tin full of yellow polish, and while his mother was polishing the floor he rubbed it all over the chairs, and the dressing-table. He took it out of the tin with his hands and he rubbed it everywhere.

He liked doing that. He said, 'Look, I polish.'

Harry's mother looked and she was so cross she shouted, *'Harry!'* – like that. '*Harry*! I've had quite enough of you for one day. You shall go straight to bed.'

And she washed all the polish off him, and put him into his pyjamas and then she put him to bed. 'Stay there you bad, bad boy,' she said. '*Don't you dare to get up.*'

Harry was very cross with his mother for putting him to bed like that. He didn't think he'd been naughty. So he got out of bed and screamed and banged and shouted till his father called out, 'Do you want me to come up there?' and then he was very quiet.

He was so quiet his mother nearly forgot all about him. When she did remember him again she went in to see what he was doing. When she saw him she began to laugh.

Bad Harry had forgotten all about being sent to bed because he was

naughty. He had kicked his legs up in the air under the bedclothes and made a little tent, and taken his Teddy and all his toys into the tent with him.

'I've made a house,' Harry said.

And he wouldn't go downstairs. He liked playing house so much he stayed on his bed all the afternoon, laughing and talking to himself.

My mother brought us round to see Harry's mother that afternoon and when my little sister heard him laughing upstairs she ran up to see what he was doing.

She liked his game so much, she went into the little house too and they had a lovely time.

'I put him to bed for being naughty,' Harry's mother said. 'I think I shall have to put him there when I want him to be good.'

9. Bad Harry and Mrs Cocoa's art-pot

Long ago, when Bad Harry was very small, he had beautiful golden curls and looked very good. Afterwards he had a haircut and then he looked as naughty as my sister did.

Well now, here is a story about the time before Harry had his hair cut.

One day, all the people where we lived were very excited because a famous lady was coming to our town.

Bad Harry's father was specially excited because he was one of the people who had asked this lady to come. Lots of people came to his house to talk about the lady's visit, and say what they ought to do to make things nice for her.

She was going to make a speech in the parish hall, and Harry's father said they must put lots of flowers in the hall to make it look pretty. He went round asking people if they would lend vases to put flowers in, and if they could spare some flowers from their gardens to go in the vases.

Our mother said she would lend some vases, and Father said he would send some of his flowers. Mrs Cocoa Jones who lived next door to us, said she didn't think Mr Jones would like to cut his flowers, but she would lend her fern in the brass art-pot.

That was very kind of Mrs Cocoa because that fern in the brass art-pot was in her sitting-room window and she liked to see it there when she came up her front path every day.

Lots of people promised to find some flowers for the hall. One lady said she thought someone ought to give the famous lady some flowers for herself. She said, 'I think Harry should do it. With all those lovely curls he would be sweet.'

Harry's father wasn't very sure

about this, but the lady said, 'Oh yes, after all he is your little boy – and you have worked so hard.'

Bad Harry's father said, 'Well, I'll ask him, but I don't think he'll want to do it.'

But Harry *did* want to do it. He wanted to do it very much.

So his father took him down to the parish hall and he practised walking up the steps on one side of the platform, and bowing and pretending to give the flowers to the lady and going off on the other side of the platform, and he did it beautifully.

He practised so hard that when the

Lady's Visit Day came he did it perfectly. He walked up on to the platform, and bowed and gave the lady the flowers and looked so good and nice that everyone in the hall smiled and clapped and the actress lady gave him a kiss.

He was Good Harry then – but oh dear!

After Harry had given the lady her flowers he had to go and sit down in the front row of the hall with his mother, because his father and the other people who'd asked the lady to come were staying up on the platform with her. So, when Harry got down his mother was waiting to take him to his seat.

Now all the seats in the hall had pieces of paper on them. They had been put there for people to read. When Bad Harry got to his seat there was a piece of paper for him too. Bad Harry picked up his piece of paper and pretended to read it like the grown-up people were doing, but he soon got tired of that and started to look around and fidget.

The people on the platform began to talk. Then Harry's father said something, and people clapped, and then the lady began to speak. Harry

listened for a little while but he didn't
understand what she was talking
about, so he began to flap his piece of
paper. Then he pretended it was an
aeroplane and moved it about in the
air over his head.

Harry's mother got very cross. She snatched his piece of paper away from him and said, 'Behave yourself.'

She snatched so hard she left a little piece of the paper in Harry's hand!

Poor Harry! He was *trying* to be good. Now he tried very hard indeed. He sat very still and stared straight in front of him.

And there – right in front of him on the platform – was Mrs Cocoa's lovely shiny brass pot with the fern in it standing among the other ferns and vases of flowers.

Harry looked hard at Mrs Cocoa's pot – and, in its shiny brass side, he

saw a funny little boy looking at him.
It was himself of course.

Have you ever seen those mirrors
that make you look all sorts of
funny shapes – they have them at
fairs sometimes? Well, that's the sort
of funny shape Harry-in-the-pot
looked like.

Harry was very interested to see
himself looking like that. He put his
head forward – and the boy in the pot
looked like an upside-down pear with
big curls on top!

Then he stuck his chin up and that
made his eyes look wavy. He turned
his head this way, and that way – and

every time he moved Harry-in-the-pot looked stranger and stranger.

It was a lovely game. Harry began to pull faces and the faces in Mrs Cocoa's pot were uglier than the ones Harry made!

And then: do you remember the little piece of paper Harry still had in his hand? Can you guess what he did with it?

He licked the piece of paper, and stuck it on his nose!

And then he pulled such a dreadful face at himself, and Harry-in-the-pot with a piece of paper on his nose pulled such a funny face back at him that he laughed out loud.

Now all the people sitting up on the platform had been looking at the lady and listening to her talking, but soon first one and then another looked down and saw Bad Harry making those dreadful faces. They began to look very shocked, especially as Bad Harry's mother was looking up at the lady and hadn't noticed what he was doing.

She didn't look at Harry until he laughed out loud. Then she looked – and so did the Famous Lady.

Harry's mother was very cross indeed, but the lady wasn't. When she saw Bad Harry with the piece of paper stuck on his nose making dreadful faces and laughing she stopped talking and began to laugh too.

She laughed so much, all the people in the parish hall laughed as well, though at first they didn't know what she was laughing at.

Harry's mother didn't laugh though. She was very cross. She picked Harry up quickly and hurried down the hall with him and then the people laughed more than ever because he had still got the piece of paper stuck on his nose!

The lady wasn't a bit cross. Later

on she told Harry's father she hadn't enjoyed herself so much for ages.

Now our mother was at that meeting, and she told us about it afterwards. She was quite shocked.

But my naughty little sister wasn't shocked. She was very interested. And do you know what she did?

As soon as Mrs Cocoa's shining brass pot was back in her sitting-room window she went straight round to have a look at it for herself, and she pulled faces at herself and made herself laugh, like Bad Harry had done!

And after that, when Bad Harry came to play at our house, they

sometimes asked Mrs Cocoa if they
could come and play 'Funny Faces'
with her art-pot, and if she had got
time, and their shoes weren't muddy,
kind Mrs Cocoa would let them!

Read more books about

My Naughty
Little Sister

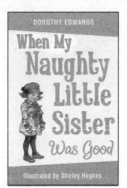

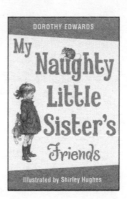

EGMONT PRESS: ETHICAL PUBLISHING

Egmont Press is about turning writers into successful authors and children into passionate readers – producing books that enrich and entertain. As a responsible children's publisher, we go even further, considering the world in which our consumers are growing up.

Safety First
Naturally, all of our books meet legal safety requirements. But we go further than this; every book with play value is tested to the highest standards – if it fails, it's back to the drawing-board.

Made Fairly
We are working to ensure that the workers involved in our supply chain – the people that make our books – are treated with fairness and respect.

Responsible Forestry
We are committed to ensuring all our papers come from environmentally and socially responsible forest sources.

For more information, please visit our website at
www.egmont.co.uk/ethicalpublishing

The Forest Stewardship Council (FSC) is an international, non-governmental organisation dedicated to promoting responsible management of the world's forests. FSC operates a system of forest certification and product labelling that allows consumers to identify wood and wood-based products from well-managed forests.

For more information about the FSC, please visit their website at www.fsc-uk.org

FSC
Mixed Sources
Product group from well-managed forests and other controlled sources
Cert no. TT-COC-2063
www.fsc.org
© 1996 Forest Stewardship Council